Rich Bye

For Mark

Library of Congress Cataloging in Publication Data
Seidler, Rosalie.
     Panda cake.
     SUMMARY: Willy doesn't get any of Mama's special
panda cake for which he carefully helped gather
ingredients.
     [1. Pandas—Fiction.   2. Stories in rhyme]
I. Title.
PZ8.3.S4615Pan   [E]   78-6109
ISBN 0-8193-0962-1   ISBN 0-8193-0963-X lib. bdg.

Weekly Reader Children's Book Club presents

PANDA CAKE

Words and Pictures by Rosalie Seidler

Parents' Magazine Press · New York

A panda cake, a panda cake,
Mama is making a panda cake.

Now a panda cake is a special cake,
It's not like any you've eaten,
It has apples and roots
And bamboo shoots
And clover honey for topping.

"But for mama to make this wonderful cake,
You two will have to go shopping."

"I'll need some eggs,
I'll need some berries,
Some sunflower seeds
And a few ripe cherries.

So here's the list
And here's the money,
And Willy remember
The apples and honey."

"Look, sunflower seeds,"

"And huckleberries,"

"Let's take these eggs,"

"And those ripe cherries."

"We'll pick some apples,"

"We'll dig for roots,"

"We'll take some honey,"

"And bamboo shoots."

"We have the fruit,
   The eggs and the honey,
   And we haven't spent any
   Of mama's money.

   So you take the basket
   And go on ahead,
   While I visit the fair
   For an hour instead.

"And you can do something
    That's just as much fun,
    You can lick out the bowl
    When mama is done!

    And while mama is stirring
    The batter around,
    I'll take a few turns
    On the merry-go-round."

A panda cake, a panda cake,
Mama is making a panda cake.

She sifts and measures
And stirs and beats,

Then adds the fruit
While the oven heats.

She whips the batter round and round,

Then bakes it all to a golden brown.

The cake is finished
It's ready to eat—
It's high and light
And not too sweet.

"But it has MY apples,"

"And it has MY roots,"

"It has MY honey,"

"And MY bamboo shoots."

"It has MY seeds,"

"And it has MY berries."

"It has MY eggs,"

"And MY ripe cherries."

So mama invited them all to have tea,
The birds, the animals, even the bee,
And everyone dined on that wonderful cake
That only a panda knows how to make.

And they all thanked Willy
When he finally arrived,
Having spent mama's money
On the very last ride.

"Thank you Willy, for taking our fruit,
Our eggs and honey and bamboo shoots,
We would never have guessed
That when mixed they would make
So delicious a treat as a panda cake."

But nothing was left of that wonderful cake
That only a panda knows how to bake,

So two crusty pieces of leftover bread
Were all Willy got from mama instead.

That panda cake was a special cake,
It wasn't like any other,
But don't ask Willy
How special it was,
Just ask his little brother.